Ways Tiny Likes To Go

Tiny Learns About Colors

CONTENTS

Tiny Tiger Learns a Lot

Adapted from Kathleen Daly's TINY TIGER TALES
Pictures by J.P. Miller

About the Alphabet

About Numbers

About Ways to Go

About Colors

Golden Press · New York
Western Publishing Company, Inc.
Racine, Wisconsin

Tiny Tiger's ABC's

Tiny is a tiger, and this is how he learned his ABC's. He ate an Apple, and that was A.

A

B

He told some secrets to a Bear, and that was B.

He paddled a Crocodile, and that was C.

He colored a Dinosaur,
and that was D.

He ran from an Elephant, and that was E.

E

He poked a Frog,
and that was F.

F

He watered his Garden,
and that was G.

G

H

He rode in a Helicopter,
and that was H.

He ate some Ice cream,
and that was I.

I

9

He danced a Jig, and that was J.

He gave a Kiss, and that was K.

He laughed at a Leopard, and that was L.

L

He saw the Moon,
and that was M.

M

He took a Nap,
and that was N.

N

He sold Oranges, and that was O.

O

P

He swam with a Porpoise,
and that was P.

Q

He sewed a Quilt,
and that was Q.

He raced with a Rhino, and that was R.

R

S

He slept in his Socks,
and that was S.

He splashed a Turtle,
and that was T.

T

He surprised his Uncle, and that was U.

He went on Vacation,
and that was V.

W

He skated in Winter,
and that was W.

He X-rayed a Xylophone,
and that was X.

X

He found a Yak,
and that was Y.

Y

He went to the Zoo, and that was Z!
Then he went home and went to bed,
because he was so tired from learning his ABC's.
You aren't tired, are you?

Tiny Learns the Numbers

Now Tiny is counting.
You can help him.
How many hats on the cat?

There is an animal in the street.
How many horns does he have?

Don't paint the flowers, Tiny.
How many flowers are there?

Tiny and the vegetables
are spilling. How many tomatoes
are going to break?

Tiny is moving. Can you name all
the things in this truck? How many
hens does he have?

Tiny is playing a tune.
How many pears are listening?

21

Tiny Tiger is counting train things.
He counts seven cars.
He counts eight toots from the whistle.
He counts nine spokes on the big red wheel.

Here's Tiny driving his own train.
Can you count ten wheels?
TOOT, TOOT! "See you later," says Tiny Tiger.

Ways Tiny Likes To Go

Here are some of the ways
Tiny likes to travel. He likes to
ride on a bike, toss in a sailboat,

zoom on a rocket,

honk in a car,

chug on a tractor,

cruise on a liner,

float in a balloon,

clop in a cart

and bounce on a camel.
Can you pretend to travel all
these different ways?

Tiny Learns About Colors

Tiny loves to paint.
Let's see what colors
Tiny uses.

He uses yellow to paint a big door.
What hard work!

He uses red to paint a barn,
and then rests in the hay.

He uses blue to paint a submarine,
and then goes for a ride.

31

Tiny mixes the yellow and blue, which makes green.

He mixes the yellow and red, which makes orange.

He mixes the red and blue
and gets purple.
Do you like his purple car?

Red and white make pink.

Tiny mixes red and blue
and yellow– and that
makes brown.

Tiny didn't paint the bear,
and he didn't paint the snow.

Can you name the striped things that Tiny has
painted? How many striped things are in
the picture?

Things Tiny Likes To Do

Now Tiny is playing.
He is playing ball with the dog.

SQUISH go Tiny's feet
in the squashy mud.

In the daytime,
Tiny likes to read
while he swings.

At night, reading
makes him sleepy.
SHHHHH, everybody.
Good night,
Little Tiny Tiger.